AUNTY PUA'S DILEMMA

written & illustrated by
Ann Kondo Corum

MnM Books
Honolulu, Hawai'i

To all the Aunty Pua's I know!

Library of Congress Cataloging-in-Publication
Data is available upon request.
ISBN: 1-56647-086-2

Printed in Korea
First Printing, January 1995
1 2 3 4 5 6 7 8 9

For information on other
MnM books contact:

P. O. Box 37095
Honolulu, Hawai'i 96837
(808) 845-8949
Fax (808) 847-6637

Aunty Pua, that portly pig,
has a dilemma that's very big.

Uncle 'Opū from Kahalu'u
Is having a birthday on May twenty-two.

My cooking's so good and I've gotten so FAT...
I have nothing to wear except for my hat!"

My 'ōpū is big, and my ōkole is fat,
I must go on a diet and that is that."

"I'll call Aunty 'Ama, the blabbermouth queen,
She'll know someone who will help me get lean."

"Pua'a Wīwī, that piggy so thin,
knows all the tricks to trim you in."

Pua'a Wīwī said, "Take daily runs
in order to trim the size of your buns."

Aunty Pua (in a momona sweat suit),
ran through the wood and ate some fruit.

Papayas, and mangoes, and guavas too...
they're 'ono, so 'ono, and good for you.

She ran on the beach on shimmering sand....
and stopped at Cousin Ferdi's Hot Dog Stand.

She puffed up the hill, and who should she see....
but old Aunty Chongy having some tea.

She stopped to chat and admire the view,
and had a cookie, a doughnut, and a pastry or two.

Day after day Aunty Pua did her run,
but she didn't lose weight and it wasn't much fun.

"Oh no, oh no, what shall I do?
It's soon approaching May twenty-two!"

"I'll see Uncle Akamai....he has heart,
He'll know what to do because he's so smart!"

"Uncle Akamai, what shall I do?
I've nothing to wear to Kahalu'u!"

UNCLE AKAMAI, BEING VERY WISE, CAME UP WITH THIS SPLENDID SURPRISE!

"Aunty Pua, Aunty Pua, you silly pig!
You're running and running, and still you're so BIG!"

"Don't you know that pigs were meant to be FAT?
Accept that fact and WEAR your hat."

"Go to town this very day,
and buy a muʻumuʻu that's bright and gay."

"But buy a size that's right for you,
And I'll see you at 'Opū's on May twenty-two."

The 'ohana all gathered at Kahalu'u
To celebrate the birthday of Uncle 'Opū.

Cousin Ferdi, Aunty Chongy,
and friends were all there....
and Aunty Pua came in
with wonderful flair.

She looked magnificent
in her mu'umu'u of gold
And her funny hat that's bright and bold.

The 'ohana all smiled and squealed with glee,
"Oh, Aunty Pua, you look great to me!"

They ate and they sang,
and they oinked through the night.

With so much aloha, everything is all right!

Some Hawaiian Words To Help You

akamai	smart, wise
aloha	unconditional love, kindness, compassion
ʻama	talkative
haupia	coconut pudding
kahaluʻu	town on the windward side of Oʻahu
momona	large
muʻumuʻu	loose, flowing dress
ʻohana	family
ʻōkole	buttocks, rear end
ʻono	delicious
ʻōpū	belly
pua	flower
puaʻa	pig
wīwī	skinny, thin

Teri Chicken

Equipment

medium mixing bowl
measuring cups
measuring spoons
wooden spoon
tongs
knife
cutting board
9 x 13-inch pan

Ingredients

1/2 c. sugar
2/3 c. low-salt shoyu
2 Tbsp. water
3 cloves garlic, minced
1 thin slice fresh ginger root, crushed
3 stalks green onion, chopped
chicken pieces (4-5 lbs.)

1. In a mixing bowl, stir together all the ingredients, except chicken.

2. Place chicken in baking pan and pour sauce over it.

3. Place the pan in the refrigerator and soak chicken several hours or overnight.

4. When you are ready to cook, turn chicken over and place pan in a 325 degree oven for 1 hour and 15 minutes. During this time, turn chicken once, using tongs.

If you prefer, chicken may be cooked outside on a charcoal grill with the help of an adult. Serves 6-8.

Haupia Pie

Equipment

small saucepan
wooden spoon
measuring spoons
measuring cup

Ingredients

1 can coconut milk (12-13 oz.)
1/4 c. sugar
3 Tbsp. cornstarch
1/4 c. water
1 8-inch prepared graham cracker crust

1. Put coconut milk and sugar in saucepan and heat.

2. Measure water in a liquid measuring cup and add the cornstarch to it.

3. Stir cornstarch and water until smooth and add to the hot coconut milk.

4. Cook on medium heat until mixture thickens, stirring constantly.

5. Cool to room temperature and pour into prepared crust.

6. Refrigerate at least 3 hours.

Serves 6.

Creamy Fruit Dip

Equipment

medium mixing bowl
wooden spoon
knife
cutting board
toothpicks or wooden skewers

Ingredients

11 pkg (8oz.) cream cheese
1 jar (7oz.) marshmallow cream
Fruit such as apples, bananas, mangoes, pears, peaches, seedless grapes, pineapple, and strawberries.

1. Soften cream cheese by leaving it at room temperature for 30 minutes.

2. Put the cream cheese and marshmellow cream in the mixing bowl and stir until they are blended together

3. Wash fruit; cut into wedges or chunks.

4. Put a toothpick in each piece of fruit OR put several fruits on skewers.

5. Arrange the fruit on a platter and serve with the dip.

Chinese Salad

Equipment

large mixing bowl or salad bowl
large fork and spoon
blender or jar
measuring spoons
knife
cutting board

Salad Ingredients

1 medium head lettuce, shredded or torn
2 stalks celery, sliced
1 small can sliced water chestnuts
1 stalks green onion
1/2 bag won ton chips (or 1/2 can fried Chinese noodles)

1. Place all of the ingredients, except chips, in salad bowl.

2. Add chips and dressing just before serving and toss together.

Dressing

4 Tbsp. oil
1 Tbsp. sesame oil
3 Tbsp. vinegar
1/2 tsp. salt
1/2 tsp. pepper
2 Tbsp. sugar

Place ingredients in a jar and shake well, or blend in a blender.
Serves 6.